JANE AUSTEN

Children's Stories

Dados Internacionais de Catalogação na Publicação (CIP) de acordo com ISBD

A933n Austen, Jane
Northanger Abbey / Jane Austen. – Jandira : W. Books, 2025.
96 p. ; 12,8cm x 19,8cm. – (Jane Austen Children's Stories)

ISBN: 978-65-5294-183-1

1. Literatura infantojuvenil. 2. Romance. 3. Literatura estrangeira. 4. Literatura inglesa. 5. Amor. 6. Preconceito. 7. Inglaterra. I. Título. II. Série.

2025-593 CDD 028.5
CDU 82-93

Elaborado por Vagner Rodolfo da Silva - CRB-8/9410
Índice para catálogo sistemático:
1. Literatura infantojuvenil 028.5
2. Literatura infantojuvenil 82-93

1st edition in 2025
www.cirandacultural.com.br

JANE AUSTEN

Northanger Abbey

W. Books

Chapter 1

Catherine Morland was an ordinary girl. She lived with her parents and her nine brothers and sisters in a cottage surrounded by a meadow.

She was neither rich, nor poor. She played cricket as much as she danced, but best of all she loved to read.

Catherine could escape for hours within the pages

of a book. She would find a cosy reading corner where her brothers and sisters wouldn't pester her. There she would travel to haunted castles, witness daring sword fights and run away from wicked barons.

Never did Catherine Morland think that she would one day be the star of her own adventure. Nothing very much ever happened to her. Until the day her parents' friends, Mr and Mrs Allen, came to visit.

'My dear Catherine!' Mrs Allen exclaimed as Catherine joined them in the parlour for tea. 'How you've grown!'

Perhaps it was the fact that Mr and Mrs Allen did not have children of their own that made it so surprising to them that years should pass and children should grow into young adults. Catherine had always been a favourite of her mother's friends, and she enjoyed their visits.

'Mrs Allen has an invitation for you,' said Catherine's mother, patting the seat

next to her. 'They are to go to Bath for a while and would like you to join them.'

Catherine's heart leapt. Bath was the most fashionable place in England. It was the place to be seen, and the place to see other people. There were balls and concerts and plays every night.

'Thank you,' replied Catherine with a big smile. 'I would like that very much.'

Chapter 2

The first thing the Allens did when they arrived in Bath was buy Catherine a whole wardrobe of gowns and day dresses. The Allens were very rich and Catherine felt like a duchess. The dresses were the first new clothes she had ever had. The rest of her clothes came via her older sisters and often needed to be mended or adjusted to fit.

The second thing the Allens did was to take Catherine to the Lower Rooms. This was a gathering place for

Bath's finest ladies and gentlemen to dance, play cards and drink tea. The only trouble was that the Allens and Catherine did not know anyone there. Mr Allen had retired to the card room almost immediately. Now his wife and Catherine stood awkward and alone. They had no choice but to wait to be introduced to someone.

'How tiresome it is not to know anyone,' said Mrs Allen. 'May we at least find somewhere to sit …' The room was so crowded that this seemed unlikely.

At that moment, the Master of Ceremonies (the person in charge of the Lower Rooms and all the people in it) approached Catherine and Mrs Allen with a young gentleman. Catherine noted the friendly smile on the young man's face.

'Mrs Allen, this is Henry Tilney,' the Master of Ceremonies said. 'He wishes to be introduced to you and your young friend.'

Mr Tilney, Catherine and Mrs Allen all bowed to each other. The Master of Ceremonies was called to make another introduction.

Mr Tilney said, 'I am very pleased to meet you. I was wondering if Miss Morland would be free for the next dance?'

Catherine flushed a little, but nodded enthusiastically. 'I am free, sir,' she replied. As the musicians began to play, Henry led Catherine to the dance floor. Mrs Allen looked on happily.

Henry Tilney was a good dancer. He was neither too rushed nor too slow, and he knew the steps without having to count or look at his feet. He was also handsome, but not in the way Catherine pictured the heroes in her beloved books. Henry's handsomeness was of a friendly sort. It immediately put Catherine at ease.

'I believe we are supposed to make conversation while we dance,' Henry said with a smile. 'Or we may be removed from the floor for impoliteness!'

Catherine laughed. 'Very well,' she said. 'How do you suggest we begin?'

Henry looked thoughtful. Then he arched one eyebrow. 'Have you been in Bath long?' he asked in a proud, formal manner.

'Not at all, sir!' Catherine replied, copying his tone.

'And do you like it so far?'

'It's delightful!'

Catherine couldn't remember a time when she'd had so much fun

dancing. Her cheeks ached from laughing.

When the song finished, Henry led her back to Mrs Allen, who had finally found two seats by the side of the dance floor. The trio chatted happily for a while before Henry took Catherine for one more dance. It was

even more fun than the last.

On the coach ride home, Mr Allen told his wife and Catherine what he knew about the Tilney family. Henry was a clergyman with a large home called Fullerton. He was the youngest son, and his family came from Northanger Abbey.

Catherine gasped. Northanger Abbey! The name alone made her imagine dark corridors and secret passageways. The perfect setting for ghostly adventures. That night Catherine's dreams were full of them – and of Henry Tilney.

Chapter 3

The following morning, Mrs Allen and Catherine were taking a stroll to a new bonnet shop. There they bumped into an old school friend of Mrs Allen's.

'Mrs Thorpe!' she exclaimed. 'How lovely to see you!'

Mrs Thorpe was in Bath with her daughter, Isabella, and they were soon to be joined by her son, John.

'John Thorpe?' asked Catherine. 'Then you must know my brother, James! He goes to Oxford university with John.'

'Why yes!' replied Mrs Thorpe. 'He and John are good friends. He came to stay with us not long ago.'

While the old school friends caught up, Isabella took Catherine's arm. 'I am so glad to meet you,' she began. 'Your brother and I got on so well when he came to visit us. I am sure that I will love you just the same!'

Catherine smiled at the young woman. She was very pretty. She had fair hair and fashionable clothes, although Catherine noticed that they weren't as new as her own. From

James's letters, Catherine knew that the Thorpes had little money since the death of Mr Thorpe a few years ago.

The next few days were spent largely in the Thorpes' company. Mrs Allen and Mrs Thorpe had plenty to catch up on. While they did, Catherine enjoyed having someone her own age to talk to and go places with. However, she always looked out for Mr Tilney at the plays or concerts they attended. She felt a stab of disappointment when he was not there.

Fortunately, Isabella was good company. She liked to talk about novels as much as Catherine. She also spent a lot of time talking about other people, fashion and Catherine's own brother, James. So it pleased both young women when he and John Thorpe arrived together in Bath one sunny afternoon while Catherine and Isabella were out walking.

'James!' cried Catherine, giving her brother a hug. 'I did not know that you were coming to Bath!'

'When I knew you had made friends with Isabella,' James said, nervously casting a glance in Isabella's direction, 'I felt I had to come. And John was very keen to meet you, Catherine.'

John Thorpe looked a lot like his sister, with fair hair and a handsome face. But as much as Catherine admired his looks, she soon grew tired of his conversation. It focussed on his new carriage and how much money their various friends at Oxford had. As James took Isabella's arm, Catherine reluctantly stepped back to walk with John.

Chapter 4

That evening saw another gathering at the Lower Rooms. Catherine was full of excitement, for, unlike last time, she now knew lots of people there. Her brother was with her (although he spent most of his time with Isabella) and

she was sure she would finally see Henry again.

As the music began, Catherine scanned the crowd. There he was! Henry Tilney was by the drinks table handing a drink to an elegantly dressed lady. The lady touched Henry's arm in thanks and Catherine felt a hot, unpleasant feeling in her stomach.

'Miss Morland?'

Catherine jumped as John Thorpe interrupted her jealous thoughts. 'Would you like to dance?'

Catherine could not say no. In truth, she would much rather stay where she was and work out who Henry was with. Instead she danced and chatted politely with John Thorpe. Catherine had to admit, she was flattered by the attention he was giving her. However, she wished it was coming from someone else.

As the dance finished, the four friends stood together to catch their breath. Catherine saw that Henry was bringing his beautiful friend to meet her.

'Hello again, Miss Morland,' Henry said with his usual smile. 'I would very much like to introduce you to my sister, Eleanor.'

His sister! Catherine nearly jumped for joy.

'Oh! I'm very pleased to meet you!' Catherine said.

'And I you,' replied Eleanor. 'My brother has told me so much about you.'

For the rest of the evening, Catherine and Eleanor chatted happily together, while Henry fetched them drinks and occasionally took Catherine to dance. Catherine tried to ignore the stares she could feel from John Thorpe. He had been forced to sit with

Isabella and James, who were so busy talking to each other that they barely acknowledged anyone else.

'Are you fond of walking?' Eleanor asked.

'I am,' replied Catherine. 'Although my friend Isabella quite hates it, unless we pass a ribbon shop or a café.'

'Henry and I were thinking of going for a walk tomorrow if it doesn't rain. Would you like to join us? We could call for you at 12 o'clock.'

Catherine agreed, and, with a lightness in her heart and step, she joined Mr and Mrs Allen to return home.

Chapter 5

Catherine woke to grey skies but she still dressed for her walk with the Tilneys. She found that at this time of year, clouds usually gave way to clear skies. At 11 o'clock, however, she spied the first raindrops striking the windows.

'Perhaps it will stop before midday,' she said to Mrs Allen. In any event, she was determined to wait for word from Eleanor before she gave up hope.

It was lunchtime before the rain had stopped, and Catherine jumped

up from the lunch table when she heard the doorbell ring. Sadly, it wasn't Henry and Eleanor. It was the Thorpes and James.

'We're going to take James's and John's carriages for a drive,' cried Isabella, taking her friend's hand.

'You can ride with John, and I will ride with James. Doesn't that sound fun?'

'I'm so sorry, I can't,' said Catherine. 'I already have plans with the Tilneys today.'

'Henry Tilney?' asked John. 'Why, I saw him and a fine-looking lady in a carriage headed away from Bath just half an hour ago.'

Catherine was confused. True, it was later than they had planned to take their walk because of the rain. However she was certain that Eleanor would have sent a message if she and Henry had decided to leave the city on other plans instead.

Isabella was already happily dragging her friend to fetch her bonnet. 'Now there is nothing stopping you."

Catherine was annoyed not to be able to ride on her brother's carriage. Since he had arrived in Bath, she had seen very little of him. He was always busy with Isabella. Instead, Catherine had to ride with John Thorpe, and listen to him chatting away about a top hat he

had spotted in a shop window. Then, to Catherine's horror, she saw Eleanor and Henry Tilney walking in the direction of the Allens' house. Henry looked surprised as the carriage thundered past.

'Stop! Oh, please stop!' cried Catherine. 'That was the Tilneys! They must be going to fetch me for our walk!'

'Sorry?' John said. Although Catherine was certain he had heard her.

'Please stop the carriage! I must go and see my friends. They will think I am very rude!' she said.

'I'm afraid the road is too busy to stop here,' said John. 'I am sure your friends will forgive you and you can go walking another day.'

Catherine was hot with rage and shame. If only she had stayed at home another twenty minutes this wouldn't have happened. If only John Thorpe would stop and let her off his carriage she could run back and explain. If only he had not lied to her in the first place!

Catherine sulked for the rest of the carriage ride. John Thorpe did not seem to notice.

Chapter 6

Catherine's stomach was in knots. She asked Mr and Mrs Allen if she could stay home from their trip to the theatre that evening, but Mrs Allen insisted that going would do her good. Their seats were next to the Thorpe family in a private box.

Catherine found that she could not return the smiles from Isabella and John as she sat down.

Catherine looked anxiously around the theatre for the Tilneys, not caring a bit for the play. She spotted them in a box opposite her own. She smiled, but Henry only nodded back, and returned his attention to the stage. Eleanor smiled weakly. The knots in Catherine's stomach tightened even more.

During the interval, Catherine jumped out of her seat to find Henry and Eleanor. Henry's face was still missing its smile. Before he could greet her, Catherine began to talk quickly.

'I am so sorry about today. It wasn't my fault, truly. My friends told me you had both left Bath and when I saw you, I begged them to stop but they wouldn't. If they had, I would have jumped from the carriage and run back to you both!'

Catherine paused to take a breath and was relieved to see that both Eleanor and Henry were now giggling softly.

'My dear, it is quite all right,' said Eleanor. 'Although my brother was a little upset. He thought you may prefer the company of Mr Thorpe to him.'

Henry looked at his sister in pretend anger. 'She is teasing me, Miss Morland. Although I must admit, it did worry me slightly.'

'Oh no!' replied Catherine. 'I would much rather spend *all* my days in Bath with you both!'

So Catherine spent the following morning with the Tilneys. She came home very happy after receiving an invitation to dine at their house with their father, General Tilney, that evening.

As Catherine was trying to decide what to wear, Isabella burst into her bedroom.

'Wonderful news!' Isabella said, dragging Catherine to sit with her on the bed. 'Your brother has proposed to me and I have accepted! We are to be married!'

Catherine was filled with joy for her brother and Isabella. It was clear they were very much in love. She hugged Isabella and tried to ignore the fact that if Isabella was joining her family, it would be even harder to avoid John Thorpe.

Isabella and Catherine joined James and John in the Allens' sitting room. Catherine hugged her brother. 'I am so very happy for you, James. Do Mother and Father know?'

'Not yet, I am going to visit them now to tell them. John is coming too. Then we shall pick out a ring on our way back to Bath,' replied James.

John took a step closer to Catherine. 'Perhaps I should pick out a ring myself, Miss Morland,' he said.

Catherine was confused. However, if John meant that he wished to buy a ring to propose to someone else, then Catherine agreed it would be a good idea. At least then she would not have to spend so much time in his company.

Chapter 7

General Tilney was nothing like his children. He was cross-looking and his conversation throughout dinner was startlingly serious. Occasionally Henry would catch Catherine's eyes and roll his own to make her smile.

Henry and Eleanor's older brother Frederick had joined them

for dinner. He looked like he would rather be anywhere else.

'Bath is full of silliness, which I do not care for,' said General Tilney. 'I am glad we shall be returning to Northanger Abbey soon.'

Catherine's spirits plummeted. 'When do you leave?' Catherine asked, trying not to sound too upset about losing her friends.

'In three days' time,' said General Tilney. 'If the Allens can spare you, would you like to join us at Northanger Abbey? Eleanor has requested it.'

Catherine reached out to touch Eleanor's hand. 'Oh!' she cried. 'Thank you! I am sure Mr and Mrs Allen will let me come.'

An excited Catherine met Isabella in town the following day. Isabella was in a bad mood.

‘I have heard from James and it seems he and I cannot marry for three years!’ Isabella cried. She had pulled Catherine into a nearby tea room, even though Catherine had much to do before her trip. ‘Your father will not give James his inheritance until then, so we would have no money to live on!’

Catherine tried to calm her friend. ‘You are still so young,’ said Catherine. ‘Perhaps Father wants you both to be

sure of your love before you marry.'

Isabella sulked as a pot of tea and a plate of cakes arrived in front of them. Her spirits only seemed to lift when a gentleman came into the café who Catherine recognised.

'That's Captain Frederick Tilney,' whispered Isabella.

'I know. He was at dinner last night,' replied Catherine. 'He seems quite disagreeable. He barely spoke a word.'

Isabella looked over at Frederick. 'He's always been lovely to me,' she said. Then, before Catherine could ask how Isabella knew him, Frederick Tilney had taken a seat at their table.

‘Well, isn’t this delightful,’ Frederick said, taking Isabella’s hand and kissing it. ‘Here I was thinking I would have to take tea on my own when I find you waiting for me.’

‘Oh, stop it!’ Isabella replied, teasingly hitting Frederick on the shoulder. ‘I was not waiting for *you.* I was here with my good friend.’

Captain Tilney didn’t even glance in Catherine’s direction. Catherine felt uneasy about the way he and Isabella were looking at each other.

‘Perhaps we should carry on with our errands, Isabella?’ Catherine said, standing up from the table.

Isabella remained seated. 'You go, my dear,' she replied. 'I can't leave the Captain to have tea all by himself, can I?'

Catherine could have said that if the Captain could command soldiers by himself, she was quite sure he could pour tea. However, she bit her tongue and left the café.

Chapter 8

As Catherine's trunks were loaded onto the Tilneys' carriage, Isabella came to say goodbye. 'What shall I do without you?' she said. 'I suppose I must make sure my brother does not get too jealous about you staying at the Tilneys.'

Catherine was startled. 'What on earth do you mean? Why should John be jealous?'

'John says you agreed to marry him the morning after James proposed to me!'

'No!' Catherine gasped. 'He asked me if he should buy a ring! I only agreed that he should if he knew someone he wanted to give it to. I had no idea he meant me.'

An awkward silence fell between the two friends. 'Would you mind telling him that it was a misunderstanding when you see him?' Catherine asked.

Isabella fiddled with the sleeve of her gown. 'I suppose,' she murmured, sulkily. 'He will be very upset, however, and I am rather busy this evening with Captain Tilney.'

Catherine sighed. She did not like the friendship between Isabella and Frederick. But she was pleased to hear that he would not be coming to Northanger Abbey.

Northanger Abbey was everything Catherine had dreamt it would be. Tall towers loomed over a deep moat and cast shadows that seemed to run for miles. The grey walls were dotted with dark, pointed windows. Everything looked cold, dark and mysterious. So, Catherine was disappointed to find that the inside was warm and welcoming.

'My mother did a lot to the Abbey before she died,' Eleanor said, leading Catherine to her room. 'I believe the love she put into this home has stayed within its walls.'

'I agree,' said Catherine. 'It is lovely. When did your mother pass away?'

'When I was away at school,' Eleanor replied sadly. 'There is a

portrait of her in her room. I will show you later when my father isn't around. He doesn't like to talk about her.'

Catherine wondered why a man would not want to talk about his wife. The more Catherine knew

about the General, the more she was confused by him. Her confusion increased that night at dinner when the General began to discuss the Allens.

'I suppose a dining room like this is nothing compared to how the Allens live?' said the General.

'Um … I believe their dining room is actually a little smaller,' replied Catherine, truthfully.

'Perhaps you have grown used to splendour, having spent so much time in their company,' the General said.

Catherine shook her head a little. 'No, I assure you.'

The rest of the dinner passed in silence. Catherine had already noticed that Eleanor and Henry were quieter when their father was around. She wondered if they might even be a little afraid of him.

The following morning, General Tilney left for business in London and a great cloud seemed to lift from over Northanger. Eleanor, Henry and Catherine played games, picked apples and went riding together to Henry's house at Fullerton. With each passing day, Catherine was falling more and more in love with Henry.

Chapter 9

'I have been meaning to ask you, Eleanor,' said Catherine. It was one morning when Henry had not yet arrived from Fullerton. 'Why does your father talk about the Allens so much?'

Eleanor looked down. 'He has heard that they are very rich, and that they have taken an interest in you,' she replied.

'Do you mean he thinks I am their heiress? That I will

inherit their money when they are gone?' Catherine could not quite believe it.

'Yes,' replied Eleanor. 'And our father believes that only one thing matters in a marriage: money. He knows how much Henry likes you and he intends to encourage the match.'

Catherine was so shocked, she could not think what to say. She was not the Allens' heiress, and she did not think she ever would be. 'Where has your father heard such a thing?' Catherine asked.

'John Thorpe, I believe. They met at the theatre and Mr Thorpe told him that you and your brother James were first in line to inherit the Allens' estate.'

Catherine excused herself. She needed to be alone for a while to think. John Thorpe thought that Catherine and James were to inherit a fortune. That must mean that Isabella thought the same thing. Was that why she had accepted James's proposal? Was that why she was so upset when their father had said they would have to wait to marry?

Catherine's thoughts came back to General Tilney. Hearing how he felt about marriage and money made her even more curious about his late wife. Eleanor had not yet shown Catherine her mother's portrait. Now Catherine found her footsteps drawing her towards the lady's room.

Catherine tiptoed inside. The furniture was covered in sheets and the floor was dusty. No one had been in this room for many months. There, above the fireplace, was the portrait. Mrs

Tilney was as beautiful and elegant as Eleanor, but her smile was Henry's. Catherine stared for a while, imagining

this warm, lovely lady married to General Tilney. She felt sure it could not have been a happy marriage. Perhaps he had even had some hand in her death …

'Catherine?' Henry was standing in the doorway. 'What are you doing in here?'

Catherine mouth went dry. 'I – I wanted to see your mother's portrait.

Eleanor wanted to show me, but she knew your father may not like it.'

Henry frowned. 'So you came to see it anyway.'

Catherine nodded.

'Do you know how upset my father would be if he knew you were in here?'

'Did he love her very much?' Catherine asked. 'He does not talk of her at all, so perhaps he did not?'

Henry came closer, still frowning.

'My father may not always express his emotions,' he began. 'But he was devastated when our mother died. Eleanor was not here, but Frederick and I were. It was the worst time of his life.'

At Catherine's obvious surprise, Henry shook his head.

'What have you been imagining, Miss Morland? What horrors do you think my father guilty of?'

Henry looked so disappointed in her and Catherine felt so ashamed that she ran to her room. At first she did not see the letter that had been placed on her table. When she eventually picked it up, she knew from the writing that it was from her brother James.

> My dear sister,
>
> I am writing to tell you that it is all over between Isabella and I. She no longer loves me and I believe she will soon be announcing her engagement to Captain Frederick Tilney. I am in despair. Beware how you give your heart, dear sister, for mine is broken.
>
> James

Catherine read the letter three more times before she could believe it. Then she slipped it into her pocket and went to join Eleanor and Henry for dinner. She hoped that Henry would forgive her foolish imagination.

Chapter 10

The following days at Northanger Abbey passed quietly. Henry's anger seemed to pass, although Catherine made sure to read fewer scary novels at night. She would not let her imagination run away with her again.

Catherine also told Eleanor about her brother's letter.

'I am afraid Isabella

must be mistaken,' said Eleanor as they walked in the pretty gardens of Northanger. 'My brother is not as careful with people's hearts as he should be. Isabella may have thought he wished to propose, but I can assure you he will not. She has no money.'

Catherine wished she could feel sorry for Isabella, but she could not. Isabella had flirted with Captain Tilney in Bath. She had attached herself to him without a thought for James. Now James was broken-hearted. It was with great surprise, therefore, that Catherine received a letter from Isabella the very next day.

My dearest friend,

I am writing to ask if you could talk to your darling brother for me. There seems to be some misunderstanding between us. You must know that I love only him, and have always been true to him. I am sure you are the right person to convince him.

With love,

Isabella

Catherine carefully considered the letter. She read it over once more as she went to bed, and decided to throw it on the fire. The sooner the Thorpes were separated from her family, the better.

'Catherine!'

Catherine woke with a start. Someone was banging on her bedroom door.

'Catherine! Are you awake?'

Catherine sleepily swung her legs off the bed. She could see a chink of grey light through her curtains. It was still early. She opened her door to find Eleanor, still in her nightdress, looking pale and distressed.

'Eleanor!' Catherine said, standing aside to let her friend enter. 'Whatever

is it? Has something happened?'

Eleanor looked at the floor. 'I am so sorry,' she said. 'I don't know how to say it.'

'Whatever it is, it can't be as bad as all that, can it?' Catherine said, kindly.

'Oh, but it is!' Eleanor looked close to tears. 'My father has asked that you leave Northanger Abbey.'

Catherine felt as though something heavy had landed on her chest.

'He has asked that you leave today, this morning, this very moment,' Eleanor continued. 'He will not tell me why, only that I should help you to pack.'

Catherine sank down onto the bed.

Henry must have told his father about discovering her in his mother's rooms. Perhaps Henry had not forgiven her after all. In truth, Catherine could not blame him.

In silence, the two friends packed Catherine's gowns, books and letters. She did not take time to brush her hair and she put on the same clothes she had worn the day before. She did not want to stay a moment longer at Northanger Abbey.

Chapter 11

Two days had passed since Catherine had returned to the safety of her parents' home. She had not explained why she had returned alone, travelling on a public carriage with strangers, only that she had outstayed her welcome at Northanger Abbey.

Catherine's mother had been furious with the Tilneys for sending her daughter to travel across the country alone.

Catherine had defended them, saying that the fault was all her own. She was miserable. Worst of all, she knew she would never see Henry again.

Of course, like most heroines in most adventures, the darkest part of Catherine's story came just before the lightest and happiest.

Catherine was about to start a game of cricket with her little brothers and sisters in the meadow beside her house.

Suddenly, her mother called to her that they had a visitor. Never would Catherine have guessed that it would be Henry Tilney sitting in their parlour, having tea and cake with her parents.

'I have come to apologise for my father's behaviour,' Henry began. He talked directly to Mr and Mrs Morland. Catherine thought he looked flustered, and his clothes were dusty from the ride.

'We *were* a little concerned at Catherine's treatment,' replied Catherine's mother. Her language had been far more colourful on the matter over the past two days.

'Had I known what was happening I would have prevented it, however my sister was the only one at Northanger.'

Henry continued to apologise, until Catherine's father stopped him. 'Now, now, let the matter rest, young man. I imagine you will need to leave for home again before the light fades?'

Catherine wanted to shout *No!* She would like Henry Tilney to always be in her parlour, drinking tea and eating cake.

‘Perhaps Catherine could show you the gardens before you leave?’ said Mrs Morland. Catherine had never loved her mother more than she did at that moment.

The younger children had abandoned their game of cricket and now came to the house for supper. Henry did not speak until they were a safe distance away. When he did it was in such a stream that Catherine could hardly keep up.

‘I must apologise again for my father’s behaviour. It turns out he had heard from Mr Thorpe that you were to inherit the Allens’ fortune.

That is the reason he invited you to Northanger Abbey to stay with us. He wanted to make a match between the two of us. You must believe me when I tell you I knew *nothing* of his plans. When he went to London, he happened to see Mr Thorpe again. Mr Thorpe told him that he was mistaken and that your wealth is not as much as it would be if you were the Allens' heiress.'

Henry paused for breath and Catherine asked, 'John Thorpe? Why would he do such a thing?'

'Perhaps because he knew his attentions to you were not returned? When Father realised you would bring nothing to the family if you and I were to marry, he ordered you out of the house. There was nothing Eleanor could do. She has been sick with guilt and worry ever since. As soon as I found out what had happened, I came to see you myself. You have done nothing wrong. You are simply not as rich as you were thought to have been.'

The heavy weight that had been lying on Catherine since that dreadful morning at Northanger Abbey seemed to lift and float away in the evening air.

'My dear Catherine,' Henry began again. 'I have no right to hope, after everything my family has put you

through. However, if you can find it in your heart, you would make me the happiest man alive if you would agree to be my wife.'

Catherine laughed and threw her arms around Henry. 'Of course!' she cried.

And so Catherine's adventure had come to an end. Or perhaps it was just beginning …